How Raven freed the Moon

Anne Cameron

HARBOUR PUBLISHING CO. LTD.
1985

When I was growing up on Vancouver Island I met a woman who was a storyteller. She shared many stories with me, and later, gave me permission to share them with others.

This woman's name was KLOPINUM. In English her name means "Keeper of the River of Copper." It is to her this book is dedicated, and it is in the spirit of sharing, which she taught me, these stories are offered to all small children. I hope you will enjoy them as much as I did.

Anne Cameron

Text © Anne Cameron 1985
Illustrations © Tara Miller 1985
Cover and book design by Gaye Hammond
ISBN 0-920080-67-7

Harbour Publishing Co. Ltd.
Box 219 Madeira Park B.C.
Canada V0N 2H0

R AVEN is the trickster.

She never uses force.

She uses her wits and her magic, and sometimes she outsmarts herself.

Raven is often good, sometimes bad; Raven is always beautiful.

Above all else, Raven loves beautiful things, especially bright, shiny things.

One day, Raven heard the people talking about an old fisherwoman and her daughter who lived on an island far to the north and had a round, bright, shiny thing they called Moon which they kept in a beautiful carved cedar box, locked away from those who might want to steal it.

Raven wanted the moon.

Raven flew all day in the bright sunlight. Heading north, she flew over the rivers and streams, over the mountains and valleys, over the trees and beach, searching for the old fisherwoman and her daughter, searching for the round, bright, shiny Moon.

Raven flew all night through the darkness. In the sky there were only pinpoints of light as the stars tried to light her way.

Finally, just when Raven thought she was too tired to go any further, she arrived at the house of the fisherwoman and her daughter.

Quickly, Raven used her magic. She turned herself into a lovely little baby girl, lay down by the door and began to cry.

Inside the cedar log house the fisherwoman stirred restlessly. Then she sat up, rubbed her eyes and looked around her house. Everything was exactly as it should be.

So she lay back down again.

Raven, who was no longer a bird, but a lovely little baby girl, took a deeper breath and cried even more loudly.

"What's that?" the fisherwoman demanded.

"It sounds like a baby," replied her daughter.

"There's no baby around here," the fisherwoman said firmly.

"Still," the daughter puzzled, "it does sound like a baby."

Raven could hear their voices. She took several deep breaths and howled at the top of her voice.

"My heavens!" the fisherwoman gasped. "It certainly does sound like a baby."

So they got out of bed, went to their door, opened it, and saw the most beautiful little baby girl they had ever seen. A little girl with coal black hair and shiny black eyes, crying and holding out her arms to be picked up and cuddled.

"Is that your baby?" the fisherwoman asked.

"No," her daughter answered. "No, it most certainly is not my baby."

"Then whose baby is it?" They stared down at the baby, who smiled at them and made soft coo-ing noises and appeared to be quite the most wonderful of babies.

"I think," the daughter smiled, picking up the baby and cuddling it gently, "I think she is our baby."

The daughter carried the baby (who was, of course, Raven) into the house and wrapped her in a nice warm blanket. "Oh, she has such cold hands and feet," she said.

"Of course she has, " the fisherwoman replied sleepily. "And she's probably hungry. No baby should sleep outside at night. Anything might happen to her. If you want to keep that baby, you'll have to feed her, keep her warm, dry, and clean; and above all keep her quiet. I am an old woman and I need my sleep. I work very hard and need my rest." Yawning and scolding, the old fisherwoman went back to her bed and fell asleep.

The daughter gave the baby (who was, of course Raven) some nice smoked fish to eat. "My," she said, "this baby certainly does eat a lot.' She did not know the hungry baby was really Raven. She probably would not have believed it if anyone had told her.

Nobody ever expects magic to happen.

The lovely little baby girl smiled and cuddled, laughed and gurgled, and ate a great deal. The daughter of the old fisherwoman began to get very sleepy, for it was, after all, the middle of the night. She made a bed for the beautiful baby girl, tucked her in, kissed her good night, and went to her own bed.

No sooner had she pulled up her covers and closed her eyes than the baby began to cry!

"What is that noise?" the old fisherwoman demanded, sitting up in bed and looking around her with fierce eyes.

"It's our baby," the daughter said sleepily.

"What's the matter with her?"

"I don't know."

"She's crying."

"Yes, mother, she certainly is crying."

"Well, make her stop!" the fisherwoman insisted. "I have a big day ahead of me, and I won't be able to do my work if I don't get enough sleep."

The baby (who was, of course, Raven) continued to cry.

15

So the daughter got out of bed, went over, picked up the baby, and sang her a song.

The baby did not go back to sleep, but the old fisherwoman did. And soon, the song made the daughter sleepy, too. So, once again, she tucked the beautiful little baby girl into her bed, kissed her goodnight, and went back to her own bed to try to get some sleep.

But no sooner had she pulled up her covers and closed her eyes than that baby (Raven) began to cry. Again.

Before the fisherwoman could even ask what was wrong, the daughter was out of bed and over to the baby.

She tickled the baby's toes.

She smiled.

She sang.

She tried everything she knew.

And that baby cried.

"Oh, for heaven's sake," snapped the old fisherwoman, "this has just got to stop."

"What should I do? She has eaten, she is warm and dry, and still she cries and cries and cries."

"Maybe," the old fisherwoman sighed, "you should find something for her to play with."

At this, the baby (who was, of course, Raven) laughed happily and reached her arms for the carved wooden box. "OH NO, baby!" the daughter said quickly, "you mustn't touch that."

The baby opened her lovely little mouth, took a very deep breath and ROARED.

"Oh, my!" the daughter gasped.

"What's that!" the fisherwoman demanded, almost jumping out of her skin.

"She wants the carved box in which we keep. . .you know," the daughter said.

"Well, she can't have that!" the old fisherwoman grumbled. "It's no toy for a baby."

The baby howled louder.

She sobbed.

She wailed.

"Wah wah wah ah-wah!"

"I can't stand any more of this!" the old fisherwoman said. "Let her at least look at the box. But she mustn't hold it herself, she'll drop it."

"Yes, Mother," the daughter agreed.

The daughter got the beautiful carved cedar box and put it where the baby could see it.

"Goo goo," smiled the baby, and laughed happily. "Don't touch it, baby," the daughter sighed with relief. "You may look at it, but you mustn't touch it."

The baby (who was, of course, Raven) lay on her side staring at the box, making soft happy noises.

The soft happy noises made the daughter very sleepy. She yawned and yawned and rubbed her eyes. She tried to stay awake.

But she fell asleep.

The baby (who was, of course, really Raven) crawled over to the carved cedar box, and carefully lifted the lid.

Inside, on a piece of soft otter fur lay Moon.

The baby reached out, took the moon in her hand, and gazed at its beauty.

She knew she wanted to keep Moon.

The bright light from the moon shone on the face of the old fisherwoman and wakened her.

"That's not baby!" she shouted. "That's RAVEN!"

"RAVEN!" the daughter exclaimed, waking.

And sure enough, there in their little house was Raven, holding Moon under one large, black wing.

"Get the Moon!" the old fisherwoman cried, jumping from her bed and racing after Raven.

"I'll catch her!" the daughter shouted.

But of course she didn't.

The old fisherwoman and her daughter chased Raven around the house, knocking over furniture, tripping over each other, getting more and more angry and upset.

"Caw, caw, caw!" mocked Raven. "You can't catch me! Caw, caw, caw!"

And Raven put Moon in her beak and flew up the smokehole in the roof.

"Caw, caw, caw!" Raven laughed. "It's mine, all mine." She flew south, toward her home, with Moon in her beak.

Through the night, which was lighted by the Moon in her beak and no longer pitch black; Raven flew swiftly over trees and meadows, rivers and streams.

But Moon is not a pebble off the beach. Moon is not a huckleberry. Moon is very large and very heavy.

Soon Raven could no longer fly with Moon in her beak. She was too tired. She was so tired she almost dropped Moon into the ocean waves.

Raven knew she would never make it over the mountains with Moon in her beak.

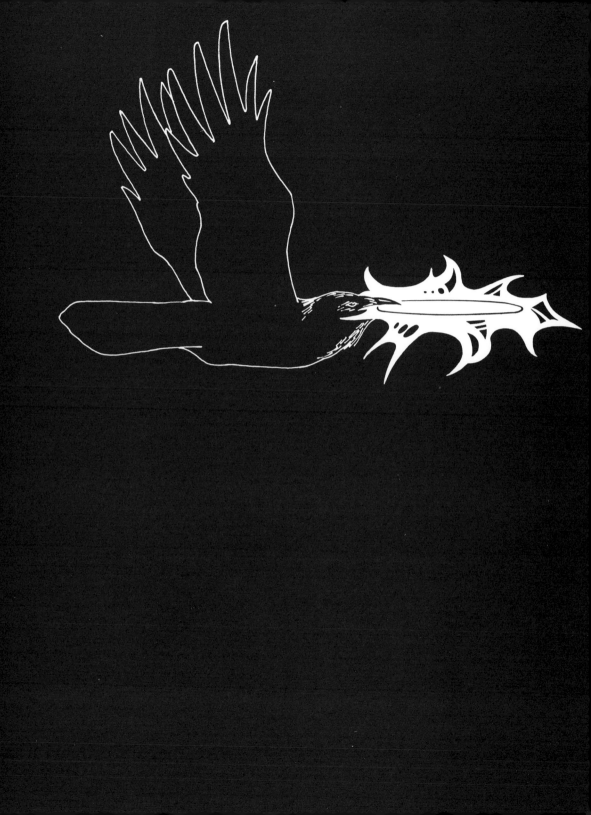

So Raven tossed the Moon up, up, up into the sky as high as she could and Moon caught on a corner of a cloud.

So high did Moon go and so brightly did it light up the sky that the old fisherwoman and her daughter saw it in their land far to the north.

"Look!" said the daughter, "look up there in the sky..."

"That's our Moon," said the fisherwoman.

Her mother smiled, and shrugged. "But look at it," she said. "Moon looks much better up in the sky than it ever looked in that box."